minnie

By the same author
UHU

minnie

Annette Macarthur-Onslow

RAND McNALLY & COMPANY
Chicago • New York • San Francisco

First published in Australia 1971 by
Ure Smith, Sydney
Text and illustrations copyright © by
Annette Macarthur-Onslow, 1971
ISBN 528–82278–0
Library of Congress Catalog Card
Number 71–123818
Designed and typeset in Australia
Printed in Singapore by
Toppan Printing Co., Ltd.

For Jason and Rachel and
the children of Loquat Valley

If you had taken the path through the woods at almost any time of the year, you might have seen a small white cat flashing through the grass, between the trees or over the garden wall.

To most of the farmers and foresters around she was known as 'that ol' white cat', or if they bothered to give her a name, Minnie. Since her master had died, some of them dropped by the cottage to give her food, and from time to time a friendly gamekeeper kept an eye on her. In her way Minnie was a princess; privileged to use the cottage by her own private 'door' and walk in the woods with the sanction of the keepers. For three years she haunted the empty cottage, her source of food and remembered warmth. But when, in the spring of her thirteenth year, a new tenant came to the cottage, Minnie with usual discretion, removed herself to an outhouse.

It was quite some time before she made friends, for Minnie's lore was to trust no stranger, human or animal. Even when she returned to the cottage and became once more a domestic cat, Minnie remained secretive, slipping away to the woods or hiding under the upstairs bed should anything disturb her. The bed was her best refuge. She hid there from the keeper and his dog; she hid from the piping voices of children; she hid from the night-prowling foxes and the hunters with their guns; and especially she hid there from thunderstorms, the thing that she feared the most.

This story tells of the crisis that took place in Minnie's life when a family with two children came to stay and occupied the whole of the upstairs, including under the bed.

I shall begin by telling more about Minnie and how she first came to the woods . . .

It was sixteen years since Minnie had been bumped over tracks in a sack and dropped out in a nettle patch. She had run through the wild unfamiliarity of the woods to take refuge in the cottage shed. She was lucky to have 'homed' on the cottage, the only one for miles around, because the Cotswold woods, deeper, darker, steeper and hillier than most, were no fit place for a very small white kitten . . . especially the terrified, trembling kitten that confronted the master of the cottage. Warm milk, a dry bed and the cavernous glow from the large fireplace soon enveloped the kitten in a safe new world, and some time later a confident young cat ventured out of the cottage garden again to sample the world beyond the hedgerow and the trees.

She soon became neat at seeking the woodland ways and moving among the animals and birds that lived there: the badgers, pheasants, deer, foxes, weasels, stoats, owls, partridges, squirrels, fieldmice and shrews. She skirted the woods through the seed-laden grass, scenting the rabbit runs and hare 'forms' and the hillocks made by the little brown moles.

She also discovered the shadowy and secret places where cats could hide. Some cats, like Minnie, had been left in the woods to fend for themselves; others had run away from home or been bred in the wild. These feral cats had joined the woodland hunters, and lived in fear of the gamekeepers and their dogs. There were tabbies, browns, greys and gingers, stealthily camouflaged in bracken and bramble, trusting no one and having no friends.

Minnie's only real camouflage was the snow, but this did not prevent her from parading the woods at all seasons. Being conspicuous did not seem to bother her—she moved through the leaves and ferns with as much disguise as a rabbit's white scut on its brown furry body.

The cottage so close to the woods was perfect for these sorties.
The entrance was barred to foxes or weasels by Minnie's private
'cat door'—a passage that led to a leather-hinged trapdoor which
Minnie could lift with one flip of a forepaw, to steal in and out
of the house.

Minnie would 'mouse' as an old man might fish, sitting stock
still for most of the day. She sat in the crook of the plum-tree
bough, willing the grass to offer a mouse.

When her patience ran out, as it usually did, she would pounce at the bough and scrabble her claws on the rough bark, flick her tail and scamper and leap, then stalk along the tall stone wall and try to fly with the dry leaves and butterflies. No one would guess that this overgrown kitten was really sixteen human years old (which for a cat is one hundred and twelve).

At night, poised delicately as thistledown, she would sit looking wise in the lamplit window.

Minnie was like the spirit of the house, moving around with barely a sound; greatly embarrassed if she rocked a chair, hardly noticeable except for the mini marks of surplus white hairs, dirty paws on sills, or one dug-up lettuce in a newly planted row.

She was, however, quite vocal at meal-times, and would plead for whatever was going at the table—like cheese without rind, or sultanas or carrots. She became very scornful if cheated, sulky for a long time if scolded. But when truly happy, which was often enough, she would purr and purr to such a crescendo that the sound trailed off to a thin little squeak.

On spring days when the sun-bright grass was yellow as butter-cups and the woods full of busy sounds of birds doing their housework, Minnie would sit in the glade, watching those small grass butterflies called Blues. Then she would up-tail and vanish into the trees with cat-like purpose.

On certain nights, around dusk, when the woods were full of little murmurs and cries, when owls hooted and rabbits squealed, pheasants cackled and badgers grunted, when the air was electric with intention of hunter and hunted, Minnie slipped away from the fireside, to reappear later with muffled meows and a mouthful of mouse. Like most hunters she needed to show off a little, even if it meant waking the household at four o'clock in the morning.

frost-flowers

More often, though, Minnie slept all night in her box by the fire. On very cold mornings, when the windows were covered with frost-flowers, she sometimes woke her mistress by a pat on the face as if to say: 'Wake up, Ann! The fire has gone out, come and light it again.' So while Ann, still in pajamas, collected wood, Minnie followed to make sure that she carried out orders.

Whenever Ann went away to London, Copper, the gamekeeper, called in to feed Minnie. But Minnie, who could hear him coming down the track, whistling to his pheasants across the fields, always ran to hide under the upstairs bed, because she was frightened of Louie, his big yellow dog. So Copper rarely saw Minnie.

One day, Jason and Rachel came to stay at the cottage. They arrived with their parents in a large car, loaded with so many belongings that they quite filled the upstairs part of the house, including Minnie's favorite hiding place, under the bed.

Minnie was so disgusted that she took off for the woods immediately. Ann saw her go, but being used to Minnie's woodland wanderings, did not expect her to go far.

In fact, Minnie went much farther than usual. She went down into the valley and up to a ridge where the trees thinned out then thickened into new woods—strange woods, no longer her woods. She descended again on the other side to a dark, steep place thick with pine trees. Sitting there among the soft brown needles and muffled bird calls, she did not notice how overcast the sky had become, nor did she see the bright flash that lit up the outside world.

Crash! A loud thunderclap shook the whole wood. Minnie leapt up, her white fur bristling all over!

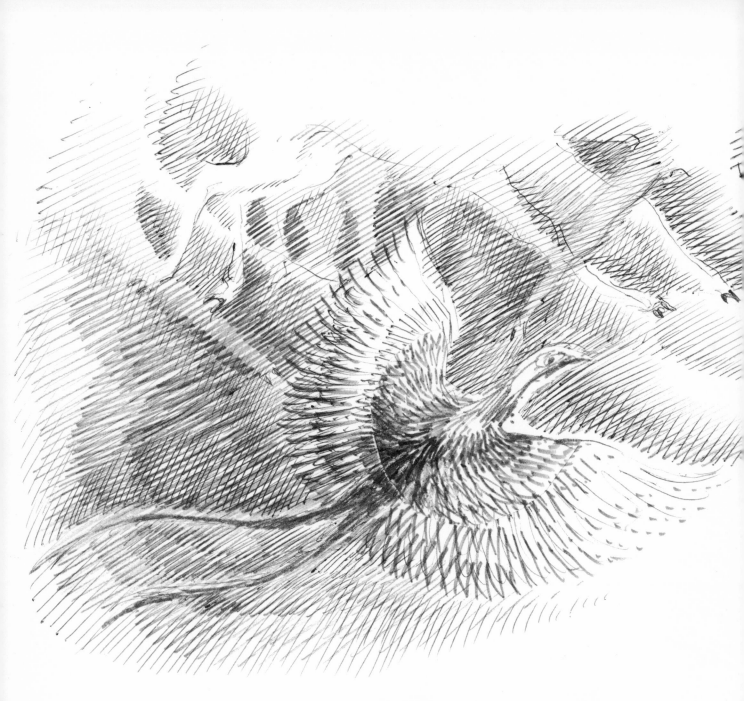

A low, moaning wind stirred the pines, and as big drops of rain began to fall, Minnie started to run, unaware of where she was going.

A pheasant cock flew shrieking into a thicket and four deer came hurtling through the undergrowth . . . the drops fell faster and faster . . . rumble, rumble . . . crash!

Minnie ran along the bank, under fallen boughs, through tangles of brambles and puddles of mud . . .

Suddenly the ground just opened in front of her . . . and . . .

Whop! She had fallen down the bank of a steep stone quarry, head-first into a nest of tree-roots.

The rain was now falling in sheets, the wind tearing at branches, and springs were opening into little runnels over the shiny stones. For five, ten, perhaps twenty minutes, Minnie crouched in the tiny cavern under the tree-roots, blinking and flinching every time the thunder boomed.

At last, when the rain eased, and the storm grumbled away down the valley, trailing the last pattering drops over the leafy floor, Minnie emerged. She tested the ground with a right paw, then a left, shaking each in turn, and then scampered up the bank and along the path towards where she thought home might be. She hadn't expected to see a sharp-faced man with a large black hound coming down the path.

It was the keeper of these woods, a mean-looking man named Tulloch, with his gun-dog Ajax at his heels. Tulloch had never seen or heard of Minnie before. Nor had Minnie seen Tulloch . . . or the terrifying black Ajax . . . . She turned to run as the keeper lifted his gun to fire, and with a 'Yip!' the black Ajax was off after her, in spite of his master's furious shouts.

29

Bramble, briar, briony, bindweed, catching, twanging and scattering droplets. Minnie fast but Ajax faster, leaping, yelping, panting and crashing. His master's shouts growing fainter and fainter.

Ajax was gaining, but seven years' training to stay at his master's
heels started to tell on him and he slowly dropped back exhausted,
his great pink tongue flopping out of the side of his mouth.

Minnie came out of the wood onto the side of a hill, a bleak and unfriendly hill with uncut corn bent this way and that by the rain, and long mounds of straw lying sodden where the harvester had cut a swathe down the center. She cat-hopped along the straw, dodging the spiky stubble, until she reached the top of the hill. Here two harvesters brooded under tarpaulins close to a blind-walled barn. The far side of the barn was open and smelled of oil and rats and musty straw. Sniffing around, Minnie found a heap of dry sacks in a dark corner. She curled up and went to sleep.

Ann, meanwhile, was worried. When Minnie had not returned by mid-afternoon, following the thunderstorm, she had decided to go and search. Jason went with her, across the glade and into the woods, down the valley and up to the ridge where the trees thinned out. All the time they called and called. At sundown when the evening mists began to thicken, they turned sadly for home.

'I shall go out later with a flashlight,' thought Ann, but she did not say so to Jason.

At dusk Minnie yawned,
stretched and peered into
the grey light. The barn
was strangely silent and
without sign of rat or
mouse, despite the strong
smell. A pale crescent
moon hung over the field
and shone in the puddles.
The curve of the uncut
corn and the rotting bales
were full of eerie black-
ness. Minnie sat for a
while in the shadow
washing her paws and
smoothing out her ruffled
tail. Then, setting out to
go back by the way she
had come, she loped like a
stoat over pockets and
pits in the straw and soon
reached the corner where
field met wood.

The near woods were sharply etched in black and grey, the lower woods mysteriously lost in mist that had rolled up from the valley stream. There were furtive rustlings, scamperings and tiny whispers. Minnie paused to trace her old scent . . . and suddenly, from quite close in the darkness of the woods, there came a series of long-drawn, spine-chilling screams . . . followed by several short barks . . . . Foxes!

In the moments that followed, two lights flashed vainly in the lower misty woods where Copper and Ann were looking for Minnie. But on hearing the foxes, Minnie was off again, over the stubble, over the straw, down the side of the wood.

Ears flattened and tail straight out behind, she fled right into the midst of a herd of deer sneaking their moonlight supper in the corn. At the sight of the flying white 'phantom', the deer scattered right and left into the wood, snapping and breaking twigs.

On went Minnie, over the ha-ha and into the next field, and there she stopped . . . blocked by a barrier of huge dark bodies, with heaving sides and staring eyes, panting great gasps of steam . . . .

Five dark steers facing her all in a row, outlined against the moon.

Steers are very curious animals—they will follow anything that looks different.

For seconds the steers and Minnie stared at each other without moving, then the little white cat backed away. She skirted the edge of the field with the steers after her, bucking and snorting and waving their tails. Fortunately they were all very fat and had short legs, so were no match for a cat.

39

On went Minnie, over stone walls, through bracken and gorse, until the hill dropped away and she slowed to a trot.

She was now on a rocky ledge, many miles from where she had heard the foxes, and a good deal farther from home. The search party, having given up for the night, were turning back, and as Minnie tended her battered paws, she could just make out the grassy bank below, before the tops of trees were lost in the valley mist. From somewhere down there came the sounds of sheep and cows and a dog on a chain.

The moon sank slowly over the horizon.

The way down was steep, even for a cat. Minnie bounced and slid over the mossy stones, down through the mist into a dank, dripping copse. She moved like a ghost, grey in a grey world without beginning, middle or end, sensing only that she was going down, that the smell of wood-smoke was growing stronger and that the pale glow ahead was becoming brighter.

The glow narrowed through the mist until it became one square patch of light . . . the rear window of a farmhouse backing onto the hillside rock. All was quiet now. Even the dog had stopped rattling his chain.

Minnie edged down the
side of the rock until the
light became a blur in the
mist again; then she felt
her way through wet
nettles along the wall,
over muddy cow-trails
and puddles to a crack in
the cowshed door.

The empty cowshed, huge and dry with sweet summer hay stuffed into nooks of its rough timber frame, was full of marvelous cat-hiding places. Minnie crawled into the straw-dry manger and fell asleep.

Towards dawn the barnyard began to awaken and Minnie, who

must have been dreaming, for her ears and whiskers were twitching, flinched in her sleep whenever a cock crowed. Suddenly there was a whistle, shrill and very close—a whistle just like Copper's. Instantly Minnie awoke and, without waiting another moment, jumped from the manger and out into the wet world of first light.

Veils of mist still hung over the valley and drops hung poised in dewy necklets of spiders' webs.

Jim, the farm boy, who had whistled his dog to bring the cows for milking, blinked and gaped at what he thought was a large white stoat hopping along by the hedge. He watched it until it reached the gate and vanished into the mist.

Lights were still on in the farmhouse, the day having scarcely begun. The dog had retired to his kennel and impatient cows stood moaning in the yard.

A hedge sparrow twittered; there were little chirpings and flutterings and bird-waking noises, and then, from the copse above the farm, the first notes of a blackbird rang out across the valley. Another blackbird joined in, then thrushes and magpies, and soon every bird on the hillside was bursting its lungs in the great dawn chorus.

Minnie was dreadfully hungry. It was nearly a whole day since she had eaten, and her adventures had sharpened her hunger. From the gate the cow tracks fanned out in all directions. Minnie followed the track that led to the stream.

Jim was the last person to see Minnie that day. The story of the stoat went around the farms in the valley, and all agreed that it must have been a cat, because it was too early in autumn for a stoat to have its white coat. Someone said that keeper Tulloch's dog had chased a white cat and that chickens were missing, and the news got around because cats are a menace, and hunters were out with their guns and dogs. These farmers had not heard of the ol' white cat called Minnie.

Ann, who had spent the day looking for Minnie, turned homeward again. 'They say there's a white cat around the Northridge farms,' said Copper. 'Northridge!' said Ann. 'That's miles away!'

The next morning there was mist in the valleys again: a mist that left the hilltops gleaming dewy wet in sunlight while the valleys remained shrouded in 'woolly blankets'. Smoke from the cottage chimney rose straight into the air, and sun touching the glass and window-ledges filled the rooms with reflected light.

Jason had been up and hopping about for ages, because today Ann was going to Northridge by car and Copper was to take him with him on his rounds through the woods. He was particularly excited because, although he had not told anyone, he had a feeling—or had it been a dream?—that he was going to find Minnie today. By the time Copper arrived, Jason had roused the whole household—including baby Rachel, who was now crying for breakfast.

Copper led Jason down through the woods. They crossed the stream and climbed to the fields. Here Copper inspected the trails, which were mostly rabbit, and pointed out places where kills had been made by a fox. There was blood and some brown and grey fur. Once or twice he showed where the deer had been feeding, where grain had been grazed or flattened on top. Pheasants flew up as they passed by the hedgerow, and a line of young steers eyed them over the top, lowing and blowing and twitching their ears.

Copper stopped to give corn to the pheasants and inspect his fox-scarers, made of clangers and rags soaked in creosote, hanging from trees. 'That's one smell a fox don't like,' he said. Jason nodded but didn't ask why, because he was secretly looking for Minnie.

Shafts of warm sunlight fell through the green rows of beech trunks, larches and firs, with the light always changing— sometimes like emerald, sometimes like bronze. Copper showed Jason how to set snares by splicing a twig with a loop of brass wire pegged to the ground with a short, stout stake.

But all the time Jason was gazing round for a cat's paw-mark or a trace of white fur.

All at once they entered the wild-wooders' wood, where the trees were dark with brambles and thickets and there was a strong, sickening carrion smell. There were cavernous burrows and badgers' setts and foxholes, and bones lying around. Overhead the rooks shrieked, wheeled and settled, shrieked and wheeled again.

'I've found a few cat skulls here,' said Copper. Jason shuddered at the thought. His hopes of finding Minnie were quickly disappearing in this dark, sinister place.

'Come on,' said Copper, 'we'll go home through the fields.' So they skirted the woods through the thick willow herb and tall grasses, purple with flowering thistles. When they arrived home Ann was there, without Minnie. 'I reckon a fox must have got her,' said Copper. No one spoke very much at lunch, and Jason kept thinking about the horrible place he had seen that morning.

Jason felt very tired after his long walk, so when lunch was finished he went to the glade on the edge of the wood. There he sat watching the bumble bees humming and the worker-bees working. The sun made him drowsy, and soon his eyes closed for what seemed a very short time.

It must have been quite a long time, though, for he woke to find that the shadows around him had grown very long . . . something was moving through the grass towards him . . . something he could not quite see.

Jason sat very still, afraid to move—and then he saw it . . . a white, furry, whiskered face with pink, twitching nose and green eyes staring at him. Minnie!

Minnie was standing there among the cow parsley and poppy seeds, ever so quietly.

He put out his hand, and for a very little moment, Minnie allowed herself to be stroked.

'Hey, Minnie!' Jason started to speak, but Minnie had dashed past him with her tail in the air, over the wall and into the cottage. Jason was running after her.

'Hey, everyone . . . . Minnie has come back . . . . Hey, Minnie . . . .
Hey, everyone!' But Minnie just purred and lapped the milk
that had been poured for her. She didn't even seem to notice
that Jason and Rachel were there. She was so happy to be back
that she purred extra loudly, so loudly that the note trailed off
to·a thin little squeak . . . .

SPECIAL NOTES

P.8 Feral Cats: Any domestic animal may revert to the wild (feral dogs, etc.). Cats adapt most easily to a wild state and grow very large, sometimes double their original size.

P.9 Scut: A rabbit's tail.

P.21 Cats usually know very well when rain is coming. Their fur stands on end and they leap and play. On this hot and listless morning, however, the sudden storm surprised everyone, including Minnie.

P.32 Corn: In England this usually means any sort of cereal crop, most often wheat. In Scotland it is oats.

P.34 Rats and mice have a strong musty smell which often lingers on after the rat-catcher has rid the barns of them.

P.37 The female fox, or vixen, has a high-pitched bark like a scream.

P.38 Ha-ha: A ditch, in place of a fence, to divide fields. (Not too many of these in the stony Cotswolds.)

P.47 Stoats are white only during the late autumn and winter. For the rest of the year they are reddish-brown, sometimes white on the under-sides.

P.52 Gamekeepers arrange feeding areas in the woods where they can tend the pheasants and chicks. They surround these areas with rags, bottles or anything dipped in creosote which they can hang from trees to scare away the foxes.

P.55 Wild-wooders' woods: The hunting or predatory animals and birds often club together in one part of the woods.